llama llama home with mama

Anna Dewdney

SCHOLASTIC INC.
New York Toronto London Auckland
Sydney Mexico City New Delhi Hong Kong

Llama Llama, morning light.
Feeling yucky, just not right.

Down to breakfast.
Tiny sneeze.

Sniffle, snuffle.
Tissues, please!

Llama's head
is feeling hot.

Llama's throat
is hurting **lots.**

Look around. Not much to do.
Trucks are boring. Tractors, too.

Make a tunnel for a train?

Fruity medicine tastes **yucky!**
Llama Llama's throat feels gucky.

Llama Llama, fuzzy brain.

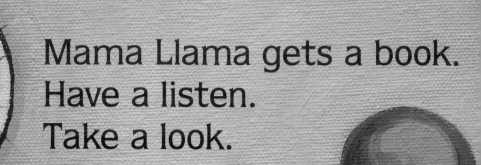

Mama Llama gets a book.
Have a listen.
Take a look.

Heavy eyelids. Drippy nose.
Llama Llama starts to **doze.**

Up again and feeling better.

Draw some pictures.
Make some letters.

Llama wants a sandwich, please!
Mama Llama starts to sneeze.

Lunch is over. Time for toys!
Mama's head does not like noise.

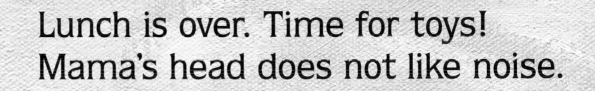

Mama makes a
big **ah-choo!**

Llama's out
of things to do.

Uh oh! Mama's throat is sore.

Being sick is such a **bore.**

Mama coughs,

and Llama yawns. . . .

How long can this day go on?

Mama shnortles, hacks, and wheezes.

Llama Llama's **sick** of sneezes!

Soggy tissues,
gobs of guck.
**Sniffing,
snorting,**

Llama Llama, red pajama,
sick and bored, at home with Mama.

WAIT! Llama Llama knows what's best.

Mama Llama
needs a **rest!**

Get more tissues.

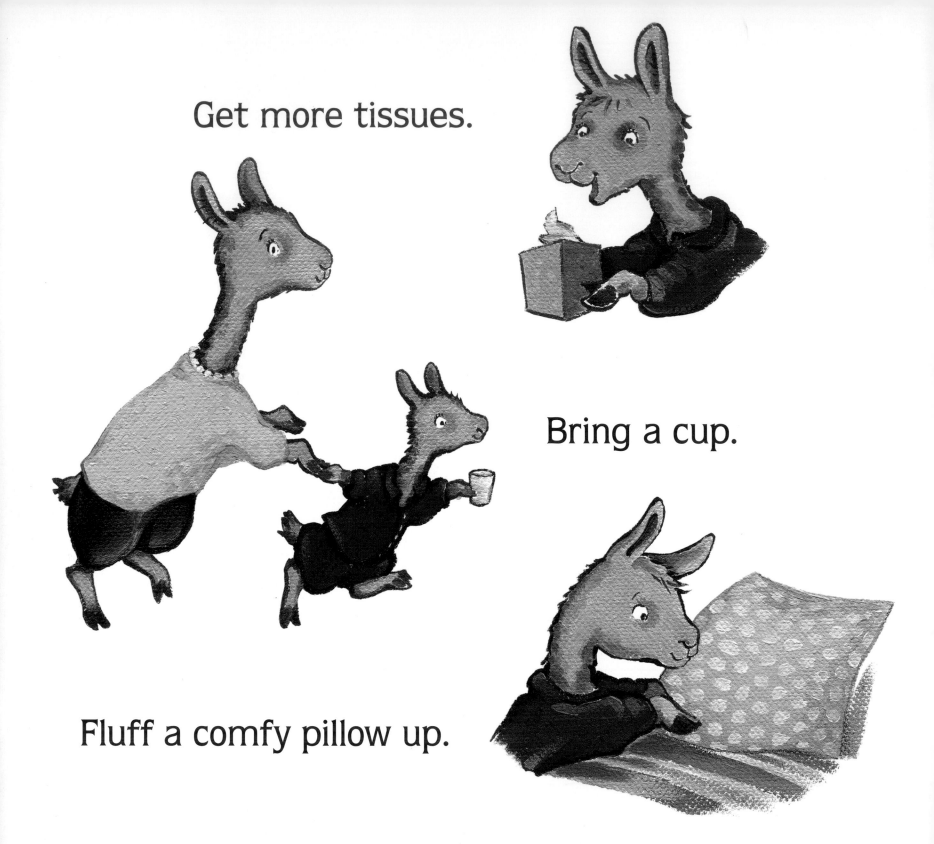

Bring a cup.

Fluff a comfy pillow up.

What else could Mama Llama need?

How about some **books** to read?